Anna

and the Food Forest

written by Stephanie Hrehirchuk

illustrated by Joy Bickell

cover art: watercolour by Stephanie Hrehirchuk

Every print copy sold plants a tree.

Anna and the Food Forest

Published by Anna's Angels Press

Anna and the Food Forest, Stephanie Hrehirchuk

Copy editor: John Breeze
Consulting editor: Maraya Loza Koxahn
Illustrations: Joy Bickell

Cover art: watercolor by Stephanie Hrehirchuk
Interior design: Colin Pruden

Printed and bound in Canada by Blitzprint, Calgary

ISBN (Print) 978-0-9958839-6-3

ISBN (eBook) 978-0-9958839-7-0

Printed on recycled paper

For Deb

"Carrots, peas, cucumbers, peppers, tomatoes…" Anna listed the vegetables she wanted to grow in her container garden. "Oh, and strawberries, Mom, *lots* of strawberries."

"All right," agreed Anna's mom. "We'll need to stop by the farmers' market and pick up the seeds, along with a starter tomato plant."

"Starter tomato plant?" asked Anna.

"Yes, tomatoes require a longer growing time than peas and carrots. It's too late in the season to start them from seed if you want to enjoy them before Christmas," joked Anna's mom.

Anna's mom had a saying: "No planting until after May-long." In Anna's city, snow could still fall in May and that didn't make for good outdoor gardening. The May long weekend was just around the corner though, and Anna was excited to grow her own garden for the first time.

For as long as Anna could remember, her mom always planted a variety of vegetables next to the raspberry bushes for Anna and her little sister to enjoy picking. But this year, Anna would have her own container for her very own garden.

She had chosen a large, round, wooden bucket with a black metal ring around its middle to hold it together, like the bucket was wearing a belt. It had black metal handles on either side. Though Anna was strong, she could barely lift the empty bucket off the ground. Once full of dirt, it would have to stay put. Even Anna's dad would struggle to lift it, and he's pretty strong!

Anna and her mom found everything they needed at the farmers' market: seeds, a starter tomato plant and soil. They even found strawberry seedlings already loaded with leaves. Anna chose the biggest one. She couldn't wait to plant her purchases. As soon as they returned home, Anna chose a location for her bucket.

"Are you sure this is where you want your bucket, Anna?" asked her dad.

"Yes," replied Anna. "It's perfect! It's the sunniest spot in the yard."

"This upper deck is south-facing," replied Anna's dad. "It gets hot enough to fry an egg out here in summer. Don't you think down near the lawn would be better?"

"I did my research, Dad," replied Anna. "All these plants love sun. Please set the bucket down here."

"Okay, but remember," warned Anna's dad, "it'll be much too heavy to move once I've filled it with soil."

Anna's dad set the big, black-belted bucket on the upper deck and went to fetch the bags of soil from the trunk of the car. Anna gathered small rocks to place in the bottom of the bucket, like her mom did with *her* plants, to help the water drain properly and not sit in the soil, rotting the roots.

Anna tossed the rocks into the bucket and her dad covered them with soil, filling the bucket close to the rim. Then she poked small holes into the soil and added seeds into each one: cucumbers on the left, carrots on the right, peas at the back, peppers at the front.

She dug larger holes for the seedlings: strawberries and tomatoes in the middle. The soil felt silky and smooth. Anna couldn't resist playing in it. She made a little garden soil man, like a snowman but with dirt.

Anna covered the seeds with soil and poured water from her favorite purple watering can over her new garden. She took a deep breath; she loved the smell of damp soil, like the smell of earth after a rain.

As the weeks of June passed by, Anna's garden grew green: green shoots of carrot ferns, green plants promising peppers, and green vining pea shoots that Anna wrapped around a wire trellis. Anna was the proud gardener of a great big bucket of green.

School let out for summer, which suited Anna just fine since she now had more time to tend to her tender plants. When July began to heat up, Anna's plants needed more water. Now she had to fill her favorite purple watering can twice a day.

Small flowers appeared, seemingly overnight. Peas, peppers and tomatoes blossomed. Small green strawberries would soon grow plump and turn red in the warmth of the sun. Anna jumped for joy. It appeared she had a natural green thumb: she was really good at gardening.

One morning, before heading off to spend the day with her family at a nearby lake, Anna took care to water her garden. It was a particularly hot summer day, perfect for swimming in the lake.

When Anna returned home, she grabbed her purple watering can and headed to her garden. Oh dear! Amid the green and white, Anna found yellow. A lot of yellow! And not the good kind of yellow. Not yellow blossoms and not yellow peppers. Her entire strawberry plant had shriveled, wilted, yellow leaves.

"Oh no!" cried Anna, as she watered the plant, hoping for it to recover. But the next morning, Anna's strawberry plant was limp and lifeless. Anna showed her mom the garden.

"Oh dear," responded Anna's mom. "Well, we can pick up another plant at the market and you can try again."

So Anna and her mom headed back to the farmers' market for a second strawberry seedling; only, this late in the season, it wasn't a seedling at all. It was a full-grown plant, with emerging red berries. Anna carefully removed the dead plant from her garden and replaced it with the new one. She couldn't wait to enjoy the succulent strawberries, already nearly ripe enough to eat.

The following weekend, Anna's family travelled to her grandparents' farm for a family reunion. Anna's grandma had an *amazing* garden. It had everything growing in it, even cauliflower. Anna wasn't a huge fan of cauliflower, unless her mom added cheese on top. There were radishes, purple and green lettuce, beets, turnips, and sunflowers taller than Anna!

Anna spent the day visiting with her grandparents and aunts and uncles, playing Frisbee and hide-and-seek around the farm with her cousins, and snacking on juicy peas and spicy radishes from Grandma's great green garden. Anna was excited for her own garden to be ready, but when she returned home to her bucket, she found another dead strawberry plant. The other plants were barely hanging on.

"NOOOOOOOOOOOOOOOOOOOO!" wailed Anna, throwing her arms up in the air and her watering can onto the deck. "Mister Sun, stop killing my strawberries!"

"It's not his fault."

"What?" Anna replied, looking toward the door. She expected to see her mom, but no one was there.

"It's not the sun's fault," said someone again.

"Who said that?" asked Anna, spinning in circles, trying to find the source of the lively voice.

"I did."

Anna looked in the direction of the sun, though not directly at it. She knew that was bad for her eyes. A rainbow face beamed at her from the sky.

"I am the angel of the sun," replied the bright beaming being.

"Wow," replied Anna, both shocked and amused. "Is there an angel for *everything*?"

"More than one for some things," giggled the angel of the sun, smiling at Anna.

"I'm frustrated," said Anna. "My strawberry plants keep dying. I guess it's too hot for them here. The soil dries up too fast and they run out of water when I'm away, but the bucket is too heavy now and we can't move it."

"Let me help you understand how plants work together in nature," replied the angel of the sun. "They use the power of community to look after one another. Some plants provide shade to keep the soil damp. Other plants provide nutrients for the soil that help the whole community grow. Everyone works together so that everyone can thrive together."

"Perhaps it's time for you to look at your garden as a community," continued the angel of the sun. "If you can help create harmony among your plants, they will all grow strong and healthy. Good luck, Anna. I believe in you."

With that advice, the angel of the sun's rainbow light retreated back into the sky and Anna quickly drew her eyes back toward her garden. She stared at the drooped leaves of the strawberry plant and the climbing vines of the pea pods. Anna had an idea.

She asked her mom and dad for help, while her little sister watched.

"Anna," said her dad. "I can't move the bucket. It's too heavy."

"We don't have to *move* it, Dad," replied Anna. "We just need to *turn* it a little."

Anna's mom grabbed one handle and her dad grabbed the other. Anna grabbed the rim of the bucket while her little sister, eager to lend a hand, grabbed a fistful of soil. Together they managed to turn the bucket just enough for the vining peas to cast a shadow over the soil without blocking sunlight from the other plants.

One more trip to the farmers' market and Anna had a fresh strawberry plant for her garden. The peas did their job of shading the soil, which kept it from drying out and helped the plants grow big and strong. For the rest of summer, Anna and her little sister filled their bellies with sweet peppers, peas, carrots and strawberries.

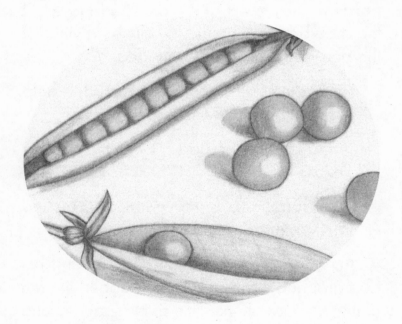

September arrived and with it came a bountiful crop of cherry tomatoes. Anna and her little sister liked to put one tiny tomato between their front teeth and bite down, spraying tomato guts at each other. An explosion of seeds filled their mouths and each other's hair. Anna's mom didn't mind, as long as they did it outside, didn't wear their good clothes, and washed their hair before bed.

September brought more than cherry tomato showers. It also brought the return to school. Anna headed back to class with her lunchbox filled with sweet, red cherry bombs.

The return to school brought all sorts of new activities, events and clubs. One afternoon, Anna came home with a form from her teacher that she was eager for her parents to sign.

"Nutrition Coalition," proudly announced Anna. "It's a group of students that learn about healthy food and teach kids in the other grades about the importance of good food choices." Anna popped another cherry tomato into her mouth. Her sister's eyes lit up.

"Not in here, young lady," said her mom, knowing what the two girls were thinking.

"Our whole class voted on the name," said Anna, swallowing the last of the sweet tomato. "Some of the other names proposed were: Health Heroes, Food Dudes, Chew Crew, Melon Heads, and Hungry Hippos. Nate suggested that one. The teacher gave him the stink eye."

"I want to join, Mom," continued Anna. "I did a great job with my garden and I want to share that with the group."

"I think it's a wonderful idea," replied Anna's mom, signing the form.

"Sounds good to me," said Anna's dad, adding his signature.

Anna spent one lunch hour per week in Miss Mujagic's class with the Nutrition Coalition team of six students. They reviewed their food groups and learned about different foods like kohlrabi and spaghetti squash, and how to prepare healthy snacks.

"Candy," said Miss Mujagic, "is *not* a food group. Though some days I think chocolate should be." She winked at the students.

Once you heard her name, Mujagic was pretty easy to say. Some students, however, twisted their tongues and tripped over the j, so they called her Miss Mumu or Miss Magic.

Anna shared stories about the plants she grew in her garden and brought enough cherry tomatoes for everyone in the Coalition. The peppers, peas, carrots, cucumbers and strawberries from Anna's garden were finished, but the cherry tomatoes just kept on coming. One pepper plant produced only a few peppers, but a cherry tomato plant could grow a LOT of tomatoes.

"Is it a fruit or a vegetable?" asked Miss Mujagic, holding up one perfectly plump cherry tomato.

"A vegetable of course," asserted Simsi.

"I think it's a vegetable," considered Jack.

"Anna?" asked Miss Mujagic.

"The fact that you're asking us this question makes me think that maybe it's not a vegetable," replied Anna, suspicious of Miss Mujagic's grin.

"You are correct, Anna," said Miss Mujagic. "And so are *you*, Simsi and Jack. Tomato is a trickster, and most people consider it a vegetable, but because it comes from a flower and contains the seeds of the plant, it's technically a fruit. Which means cucumbers, squash, pumpkins and many other vegetables are also *technically* the fruits of the plants."

"A gardener, however," she continued, "may consider the tomato and all his seasonal friends as vegetables, while the true fruits grow on trees and shrubs that return again next summer, like raspberries and apples. Generally, we treat it and eat it as a vegetable." And she popped the cherry tomato in her mouth.

"I have good news for you," continued Miss Mujagic once she'd swallowed. "Next week we're going on a field trip. We have a sister school across the city and we'll be sharing a nutritious recipe with their Grade 4 class. This week we'll decide which recipe to share with them." Anna was so excited.

The whole team agreed on Overnight Oats as their recipe. They spent their class time making a list of the materials, ingredients and amounts required to feed thirty Grade 4 students. Miss Mujagic bought everything they needed with money set aside by the school. The following Tuesday, the Nutrition Coalition went into action. They boarded the school van and headed off across the city.

In the van, Anna chatted with her friend, Rosa. The drive seemed to take forever, and the girls began to run out of things to talk about, so Anna gazed out the window. The neighborhood didn't look much like Anna's. For one thing, the houses were smaller than those in Anna's neighborhood and they were attached together in long rows. There were no garages at the front and many of the fences were in desperate need of paint and repair.

The van pulled up in front of a school and the team got out. The front doors were locked. Miss Mujagic pressed a button and announced herself. Anna heard buzzing and then a loud click. Miss Mujagic opened the door.

The team was met by Mr. Ryan, the Grade 4 teacher. He led the Nutrition Coalition down a long hall and into a classroom. Mr. Ryan introduced his class to the Nutrition Coalition and the Nutrition Coalition introduced themselves to Mr. Ryan's class.

"Alex," said Mr. Ryan, "please get the whiteboard markers for Miss Mujagic's team." Alex, a lanky boy with curly black hair, handed several different colored markers to Anna, who had been appointed to write the recipe where everyone could see it.

"Thanks," said Anna.

"You're welcome," replied Alex, smiling at Anna. "You'll want to use the green one. It writes best. The others are kinda dried out."

"Oh, okay," replied Anna. She turned to the white board to write the recipe for Overnight Oats while Miss Mujagic asked the class nutrition questions.

"Who knows which food group applesauce belongs to?" she asked.

A few children raised their hands.

Overnight Oats	
Ingredients	Instructions
oats applesauce water optional raisins cinnamon	1. Fill jar halfway with oats 2. Fill the rest of the way with applesauce 3. Top with water and stir carefully 4. Put on the lid and place in the fridge overnight 5. Eat for breakfast or pack in lunch for snack

"Yes?" Miss Mujagic pointed to a girl with a long, blond ponytail.

"Breakfast?" the girl asked.

"No, not breakfast. Breakfast is not a food group," replied Miss Mujagic. "Anyone else?"

"Grains?" hoped a boy in an orange t-shirt seated near Mr. Ryan.

"It's actually fruits and vegetables," replied Miss Mujagic. "Applesauce comes from apples, which are fruit."

Anna had stopped writing the recipe. She just stood there, holding the bright green marker in her hand. She was confused.

The school looked like Anna's school. The classroom looked like Anna's classroom. The kids looked like the kids in Anna's class. Except these Grade 4s didn't know much about food.

Miss Mujagic described the steps to make Overnight Oats as members of the Nutrition Coalition team helped students prepare the recipe, which Anna quickly finished writing on the board. She walked over to Miss Mujagic who was speaking quietly with Mr. Ryan.

"These kids don't get a lot of fresh fruits and vegetables," said Mr. Ryan. "Fast food is cheaper and, since many of our school families are lower income, fast food is usually what's for dinner."

"We do have a pretty good snack program here at the school," he continued, "but when the kids are on holidays, without the school snack program, some of them go hungry. The food bank has helped us out and we have sponsors for a sandwich-making program before winter break, but it can be tough for these kids."

Anna's feet felt glued to the floor. She stood there unable to move. She didn't know how to process what Mr. Ryan had just said. *Some of them go hungry?*

On the ride back to Anna's school, Anna didn't chat with Rosa. She sat quietly, staring out the window. Her mind travelled faster than the school van. *How can these kids not have enough to eat? How can they not know about fruits and vegetables? After all, they grow in the ground and on trees, where everyone can see them!*

Anna stared out the window of the van, which was passing an enormous school field. The field seemed to go on forever. Then the van passed another school, connected to the first school by the large field. Another field stretched from the far side of the second school toward yet *another* school, surrounded by even more grassy field.

Anna was surprised by the size of the open grassy area that these three schools occupied. It was larger than a whole, big city block. *How much soccer can a school play?* Thought Anna. *Why else would you need so much open space?*

The words *open space* echoed in Anna's head. Then her mouth began to move as fast as her mind.

"Miss Mujagic!" Anna blurted out so loud and quick that Miss Mujagic jumped from her seat.

"What is it, Anna?" said Miss Mujagic, looking as if she was ready to put out a fire.

"It's not right that those kids, like Alex, don't have enough food," said Anna.

"They have *huge* fields," Anna continued, her words picking up speed. "Apples grow on trees. Fruits and veggies grow in gardens. We can plant a food forest on some of that sports field. It can be big enough to provide fruits and veggies for snacks for all three schools. I grew enough cherry tomatoes to feed a whole class, you know. Kids can have outdoor class where they learn to grow their own food."

Anna's eyes widened as more ideas bubbled up from her brain. "In summer, students can take turns watering and caring for the garden. That way, they can take home peas, carrots and raspberries for fresh snacks."

Anna grew more excited as her inspiration and vision grew. "They could have a fall harvest party and learn things like how to make jam and canned fruit. My grandma still does that, you know."

"In fact!" Anna was nearly yelling with excitement by now, "Grandmas and Grandpas could come to the school and teach the kids how to make preserves like pickles ... and jam ... and applesauce ... and pies!"

There was no stopping Anna's steam train of excitement. "It's *so* simple, Miss Mujagic. *Every* school should have a food forest!"

"I love your enthusiasm, Anna," Miss Mujagic finally got a word in, "and I share your concern. But while it may *seem* simple, there is a lot of work required to create something that big."

"For starters, I'd need to contact the school board for approval," she continued, "and the city for land approvals and designation ... permits ... volunteers ... gardening society..."

Suddenly Anna remembered the angel of the sun's words: "Everyone works together so that everyone can thrive together."

"We could make it a team project. A class project. A school project. A city project!" interrupted Anna. "Isn't that a more important goal than teaching the food groups to someone who doesn't have any food?"

"I suppose we could investigate the steps involved," replied Miss Mujagic, looking both curious and a little excited. "It would certainly be a legacy project. Let me speak with Principal White and see what she has to offer."

Back at school, Miss Mujagic met with Principal White. Anna watched intently through the office window as they spoke. Miss Mujagic looked even more excited than she had in the van. Principal White began to look excited too. She was impressed with Anna's enthusiasm, and willing to do her part to help the Nutrition Coalition undertake its biggest project yet.

Nutrition Coalition
At Work

In the weeks that followed, Mrs. White contacted Mr. Bradley, the principal of Mr. Ryan's school. Mr. Bradley and Mrs. White contacted the school board, who in turn contacted the city planning department, who contacted the mayor, who contacted local community organizations. Anna and the Nutrition Coalition team contacted the head of the community garden program in their neighborhood. Local gardeners and tree farmers were asked for donations, and the Coalition began fundraising.

People in the community donated items for a silent auction. There were gift certificates to restaurants, paintings of flowers, baskets of goodies, hockey tickets, movie and theatre passes, and even dog grooming. Then, students hired themselves out to do odd jobs for family and friends. The money went toward the food forest. Anna's grandmother paid her forty dollars to wash all her windows. It took Anna over two hours but it was worth it.

By the end of winter, all of the approvals were in place and fundraising was complete. Spring was coming and plans for planting were in progress.

"Remember," Anna warned Miss Mujagic, "no planting veggies before May-long."

Miss Mujagic smiled at Anna. "I think the garden is in good hands with these experts."

When the time came to plant, Anna's entire school bussed over to their sister school. All the kids poured out onto the great field. Miss Mujagic chatted with Mr. Ryan, Mrs. White visited with Mr. Bradley, and Anna smiled at Alex. Teams of volunteers, mainly parents led by the local gardening communities, built vegetable planters while large machines dug holes for the fruit trees.

Apple tree saplings and haskap berry bushes, also called honeyberry, were donated by a local plant nursery. It would take a few years before they would be mature enough to produce fruit, but the vegetable gardens and raspberry bushes would provide a nice supply of nourishment while they waited for the trees to grow big and strong.

While the volunteers worked the field, the students planted strawberries and cherry tomatoes in the container gardens, along with lemon balm, thyme, basil, and dill for pickles of course. Anna was in awe of the size and energy of the community and how many people had come together to make this food forest happen. It was quite a sight!

Students looked overjoyed as they dug in the dirt, planted seedlings and filled watering cans. Teachers looked like students: grins on their faces, sleeves rolled up, elbows-deep in dirt. Alex looked delighted as he carefully put the finishing touches on his garden soil man.

Over the summer, students took turns watering the plants and enjoying all of the tasty treats that were ready to eat. The garden overflowed with fat pea pods, bright bell peppers, crisp cucumbers, carrots popping right up out of the soil, and, of course, sweet strawberries.

The best feast of all though, came in September from Anna's favorite fruit...

...or is it a vegetable?

Meet Stephanie Hrehirchuk

I wrote Anna and the Food Forest after I volunteered to help a friend's nutrition organization teach Grade 4 students how to prepare overnight oats in a classroom in Calgary, Alberta. I was shocked to discover that many of the students had little access to fresh foods. When I left the school, I couldn't help but notice the immense size of the grass sports fields around the school, and what a huge benefit a food forest would be for the students. I am happy to report that my nutrition friend is working to bring the school its first garden.

Meet Joy Bickell

Not until my later years did I discover drawing. My passion for it flowed and I knew in my heart that I was going in the right direction. One day Stephanie's father mentioned to her that he knew of someone that could draw, and she phoned me! I enjoy the excitement of drawing Anna's adventures, bringing the story to life and portraying the very important messages of Mother Earth!

Also by
Stephanie Hrehirchuk

Anna and the Earth Angel

Anna and the Tree Fort

Be on the lookout for:

Anna and the Christmas Tree

Anna's Lost and Found